Khalil's Clothes

Written by Megan Borgert-Spaniol

Illustrated by Lisa Hunt

GRL Consultant Diane Craig,
Certified Literacy Specialist

Lerner Publications ◆ Minneapolis

Note from a GRL Consultant

This Pull Ahead leveled book has been carefully designed for beginning readers. A team of guided reading literacy experts has reviewed and leveled the book to ensure readers pull ahead and experience success.

Lerner Publications
An imprint of Lerner Publishing Group, Inc.
241 First Avenue North
Minneapolis, MN 55401 USA

For reading levels and more information, look up this title at www.lernerbooks.com.

Main body text set in Mikado 24/41
Typeface provided by Hannes von Doehren.

The images in this book are used with the permission of: Lisa Hunt

Library of Congress Cataloging-in-Publication Data

Names: Borgert-Spaniol, Megan, 1989– author. | Hunt, Lisa (Lisa Jane), 1973– illustrator.
Title: Khalil's clothes / written by Megan Borgert-Spaniol ; illustrated by Lisa Hunt.
Description: Minneapolis : Lerner Publications, [2023] | Series: My world (Pull ahead readers. Fiction) | Includes index. | Audience: Ages 4–7. | Audience: Grades K–1. | Summary: "Khalil wears different outfits for his daily activities. With decodable text and color illustrations, young readers can learn about kinds of clothes. Pairs with the nonfiction title Clothes We Wear"— Provided by publisher.
Identifiers: LCCN 2022008690 (print) | LCCN 2022008691 (ebook) | ISBN 9781728475882 (lib. bdg.) | ISBN 9781728478807 (pbk.) | ISBN 9781728483580 (eb pdf)
Subjects: LCSH: Readers (Primary) | Clothing and dress—Juvenile fiction. | LCGFT: Readers (Publications)
Classification: LCC PE1119.2 .B67484 2023 (print) | LCC PE1119.2 (ebook) | DDC 428.6/2— dc23/eng/20220310

LC record available at https://lccn.loc.gov/2022008690
LC ebook record available at https://lccn.loc.gov/2022008691

Manufactured in the United States of America
1 – CG – 12/15/22

Table of Contents

Khalil's Clothes

Khalil wears his robe
at breakfast.

Khalil wears a shirt
for school.

At school Khalil plays soccer. "We wear shorts for soccer," he said.

After school Khalil goes to karate.

"I wear a yellow belt,"
he said.

Khalil wears his sweater
at dinner.

13

Khalil puts on pajamas
for bed.

"Good night!" he said.

What is your favorite piece of clothing?

Did You See It?

pajamas

shirt

shorts

Index